21st Century Skills Library

COOL ARTS CAREERS

MUSICIAN

BARBARA A. SOMERVILL

Published in the United States of America by
Cherry Lake Publishing Ann Arbor, Michigan
www.cherrylakepublishing.com

Content Adviser
Heejin Weisbrod, Violinist, Virginia Symphony Orchestra

Photo Credits
Cover and page 1, ©iStockphoto.com/quavondo; page 4, ©Pavalache Stelian/Dreamstime.com; page 8, ©David Mark/Dreamstime.com; page 9, ©Tatiana Morozova/Dreamstime.com; page 10, ©iStockphoto.com/stray_cat; page 13, ©iStockphoto.com/CEFutcher; page 14, ©Joel Stuthman/Alamy; page 16, ©Vonora/Dreamstime.com; page 19, ©Frances Roberts/Alamy; page 21, ©Pcruciatti/Dreamstime.com; page 22, ©Ahmet Ihsan Ariturk/Dreamstime.com; page 25, ©photolibrary. All rights reserved; page 26, ©Yulia Trunina/Dreamstime.com; page 28, ©Andrew Cowie/Alamy

Library of Congress Cataloging-in-Publication Data
Somervill, Barbara A.
Musician/by Barbara A. Somervill.
p. cm.—(Cool arts careers)
Includes bibliographical references and index.
ISBN-13: 978-1-61080-132-4 (lib. bdg.)
ISBN-10: 1-61080-132-6 (lib. bdg.)
1. Music—Vocational guidance—Juvenile literature. 2. Music Trade—Vocational guidance—Juvenile literature. I. Title. II. Series.
ML3795.S635 2011
780.23—dc22 2011000167

Cherry Lake Publishing would like to acknowledge the work of The Partnership for 21st Century Skills. Please visit *www.21stcenturyskills.org* for more information.

Printed in the United States of America
Corporate Graphics Inc.
July 2011
CLFA09

COOL ARTS CAREERS

MUSICIAN

TABLE OF CONTENTS

CHAPTER ONE

A DAY AT WORK

A musician is anyone who makes music. That person can be a rock guitarist, an opera singer, a piano teacher, a **composer**, or a **conductor**. Musicians can play pianos

Becoming and staying a successful musician requires a lot of practice.

or piccolos. They may sing hymns in a church or "Take Me Out to the Ball Game" in a ballpark. Some musicians become stars and make millions of dollars. Most do not. But they do work in a variety of rewarding musical jobs. They play because music is the thing they love most. Music is not just a living. It is a life.

✦✦✦

Tasha George-Hinnant runs through her finger exercises at the piano. **Scales** come first. She plays with her left hand, then her right hand, and then both hands together. Finger and hand strength are important for professional pianists. Tasha is a recent college graduate and a professional musician. She has years of experience playing piano. But she still takes lessons and practices often. "Practice," she says, "is less about the time you spend and more about consistency and quality."

Tasha's teacher is known around the world. He is helping her prepare a piece for an **audition**. Tasha hopes the audition will win her a place in graduate school, where she wants to get a master's degree in **performance** piano. Tasha also teaches private piano lessons to children. "Teaching private lessons is a musician's bread and butter," she says. "Lesson fees pay the bills."

21ST CENTURY CONTENT

Music therapy uses music to improve the mental and physical health of patients. People have been using it for hundreds of years. It has recently become popular around the world, though. Research shows that music helps people heal faster, manage stress, and relax. Music therapists work with people who have conditions such as Alzheimer's disease, cancer, and autism. Music increases brain activity, reduces heart rates, and eases breathing. Professional music therapists must study both music and psychology.

✦✦✦

Elliott Smith teaches choir, classical piano, and history of piano literature at a small college in Cincinnati, Ohio. He also gives private music theory lessons, but his real love is conducting. "Being a concert pianist is a lonely profession," he says. "You practice by yourself. You play by yourself." Smith prefers working with others. That is why conducting excites him. "Conducting lets me work with other musicians," he explains.

Recently, Smith received a **grant** to conduct a Bach piece with professional musicians. He put hours of work into learning each part and understanding how they came together.

The grant was small. Smith could only afford to pay the musicians for 1 hour of **rehearsal** and their time onstage. By the end, he had spent more than 60 hours preparing for a single 25-minute performance.

✦✦✦

A U.S. Army sergeant polishes his boots, brass buttons, and trumpet. He's been up since the crack of dawn. Like other soldiers, he wakes up early for physical training. This sergeant is no average soldier, though. He is also a professional musician. Twelve years ago, he auditioned for a place in a U.S. Army band. He has been playing trumpet for the military ever since.

Normally, military bands play at graduation ceremonies on base. These ceremonies include graduations from basic training,

LIFE & CAREER SKILLS

If you want a career in music, see if your state has a Governor's School for the Arts. These programs allow students to specialize in music and arts studies during high school. Other states also offer summer music programs. Governor's Schools give students a solid background in music study and prepare them for a future in the profession.

cooking school, and many other training events. Army bands play **gigs** around the world. This particular day, the band is rehearsing for a Fourth of July concert being held in Washington, DC. The sergeant played at last year's Fourth of July concert, too. But he is still excited to play for an audience of thousands. He travels around the world, plays music, and earns a regular paycheck. He leads the life that many beginning musicians dream of as they begin their careers.

An army band plays for a military parade.

A conductor leads an orchestra.

CHAPTER TWO

DAILY PRACTICE

Music is an odd business. Some musicians do not need any formal schooling. Others need college degrees in order to succeed. An opera singer may not go

A person's voice matures, or changes, as he or she grows older.

to a regular college. But he or she would probably attend voice school or work with a voice coach for years before performing onstage. Many singers may not have fully mature voices until they are in their thirties. In the meantime, they train endlessly.

Some musicians teach themselves how to play their instruments. Others learn by playing with family members or friends. Many take professional lessons. No matter how they learn to play, all professional musicians spend much of their time practicing.

LIFE & CAREER SKILLS

Churches offer many jobs for professional musicians. They can also be a great place to make a difference. Compton, California, was once best known for gang activity. This began to change when Reverend Michael J. T. Fisher founded Voices of Destiny. This church-based gospel choir features young adults between the ages of 18 and 28. Many were once gang members, convicts, or addicts. Members must give up all connection to drugs and crime to join the choir.
In 2010, Voices of Destiny was named the best church choir in the United States.

Most musicians begin learning their instruments at about 6 years old. Many start even earlier. This is because basic musical skills are easiest to learn at a young age. Many children learn several different instruments. "Piano and voice are important if you hope to teach music in a school, and guitar is good for music therapists," says Tasha George-Hinnant. School music teachers need to know the basics of playing many different instruments.

"No matter what instrument you play," says Elliott Smith, "pay attention to the fundamentals . . . and develop solid, basic skills." Smith also recommends listening to many different kinds of music. Students interested in playing rock should also listen to jazz, classical, and bluegrass. Being able to understand

21ST CENTURY CONTENT

Young musicians do not often think about the military when they think about careers in music. But they should. Each branch of the U.S. military has several bands. These bands travel around the world and earn steady paychecks. Musicians must audition to earn places in the bands. There are roles for everyone from bass guitarists to conductors to opera singers.

Many schools have programs to introduce students to playing and singing music.

and play many kinds of music creates better chances to make money as a musician.

George-Hinnant and Smith both decided to pursue music careers at the age of 15. "If you intend to go to a college or music school, you need to audition," says George-Hinnant. "You can't work up a good audition piece in a week. It takes months of practice to fine-tune your skills." Preparing for a professional career can also mean learning multiple instruments, working small jobs to get experience, and developing business skills.

Music school students can take classes to develop their skills with different instruments and styles of music.

Do you need a college degree to be a professional musician? The answer is yes, if you want to teach or pursue classical music. There are 615 music schools in the United States. Interested students should look for one that specializes in the instrument or type of music they want to study. Pop, rock, and country musicians do not usually need college degrees. All musicians, however, need to understand basic business practices such as accounting, tax law, and contract law.

Not everyone can be a performing musician. Not all music lovers have star-quality talent. But there are many jobs in the music industry for people who do not sing or play.

Every performance or recording relies on people working behind the scenes. Public relations specialists, booking agents, recording technicians, instrument repair experts, sound mixing engineers, and even electricians are all important parts of making music.

Touring groups need drivers or pilots to help them travel. They also need workers who can set up, break down, and take care of musical equipment. They need advertising agencies to promote their work. Radio stations need DJs, announcers, and technicians. Many colleges and music schools have music libraries. They hire music librarians.

Technology continues to change the music industry. Music software is created by programmers who understand music. Engineers design better speakers, amplifiers, and instruments. You can work in the music industry without ever playing a note of music.

CHAPTER THREE

THE DEMANDS OF BEING A MUSICIAN

Don't try to make a career of music unless you really love it. "I can't imagine doing anything else, but it

Some musicians find work playing at festivals or outdoor concerts.

is such hard work," says Elliott Smith. In the United States, about half of the people who earn their living as musicians or singers work for themselves. This means they need to advertise their talent, find work, and pay taxes. They also need to arrange transportation, keep a schedule, and collect their fees. On top of that, they still need to find time to practice and learn new songs.

Most musicians work nights and weekends. Many get part-time day jobs to help pay their bills. Most musicians also travel often. Some tour the world. Others play gigs in clubs throughout their states or regions. Traveling can be expensive. The costs of hotels, rental vehicles, and food can quickly add up.

21ST CENTURY CONTENT

There is a battle going on between musicians and pirates. The battle is not taking place on the high seas, though. It is happening on the Internet. Music is protected by copyrights. This means the people who write or record the music own the rights to it. Some people put this music online for others to download illegally. This theft is known as piracy. Piracy has a major impact on musicians and songwriters. They cannot make money from pirated music. Pirated music costs them millions of dollars of income every year.

Musicians also need insurance to protect their instruments against damage, loss, or theft. Professional musicians need to figure out exactly how much to charge for their gigs so they don't lose money.

Competition is heavy in the music industry. A singer looking for a spot in a **Broadway** musical must audition and be chosen over hundreds of other singers who audition for the same spot. The same is true for orchestra or band musicians, composers, and conductors. Many musicians face long periods without work. They must find small jobs to fill these gaps.

Some musicians can make millions of dollars. But the average professional musician does not. Half of all musicians

21ST CENTURY CONTENT

Many musicians belong to **unions**. Advantages of being a union member include getting help setting and collecting fees and creating contracts. Unions can also help with tax advice and health insurance. They also make sure that their members make a minimum amount of money. In certain cities, unions might also help freelancers find gigs. Being a musician is a business. Members get sound business advice from their unions.

Children line up to audition for a role in the musical Billy Elliot.

earn between $11.49 and $36.36 an hour. A pianist might get $200 for playing 45 minutes at a wedding. Spread that amount over the time it took to learn and practice the songs, and the pay rate is about $25 per hour. Twenty-five dollars an hour sounds great. Multiply it by 40 hours a week and 50 weeks a year, and you have $50,000 yearly. Unfortunately, most musicians do not work 40 hours a week. They may have months of unemployment. They also have to pay taxes, union dues, transportation costs, and housing costs. Twenty-five dollars an hour is a lot less than it seems!

About half of all music directors, conductors, and composers earn between $26,480 and $63,200 per year. The lowest 10 percent earn less than $16,000. The highest 10 percent earn more than $107,000. Full-time college music professors earn an average of $80,000 per year. One advantage of a teaching job is that it pays a yearly salary. Professors can earn extra money during the summer months.

Lead singers and solo musicians earn more than those who sing in a chorus or play in a band or orchestra. Groups that can fill a large auditorium with listeners usually get paid more than musicians who play in nightclubs or restaurants. The average self-employed musician may have dozens of different jobs each year. Pay depends on the type of job. For many professional musicians, the most reliable jobs are teaching private music lessons and directing church music.

Musicians often play gigs at night.

CHAPTER FOUR

A FUTURE IN MUSIC

So you are going to be a professional musician. You might play at weddings, funerals, parties, and business events. You might sing jingles for TV commercials. Cruise

Some musicians travel to major cities to find positions in orchestras.

lines and resorts hire musicians regularly. You could get paid to play and travel. You might land a job playing for the traveling company of a major musical. If so, you would play or sing for 3 days in one place. Then you would hop on a bus and travel overnight to the next theater for another 3 days of performances.

Major cities attract musicians hoping to make it big. If there is no work where you live, you might need to think about moving. New York City, Chicago, Las Vegas, and Los Angeles are all major players in the music industry. Nashville is the center of the country music industry. New Orleans is the heart and soul of jazz. It costs more to

LIFE & CAREER SKILLS

Finding work is an important part of being a professional musician. Today's musicians use the Internet to pick up jobs. Do a search for music jobs on the Internet. Post videos of your songs on Internet bulletin boards. Develop a Web page or personal profile that potential employers can find easily. Being able to use the Internet wisely is a key part of finding gigs.

live in a city than it does to live in a smaller town. You will need more work to pay your bills.

Being a professional musician sounds romantic and exciting. But it is also discouraging sometimes. "You have to be prepared for rejection," says Elliott Smith. "You audition repeatedly but don't get a job. It is not that your work is not good or even excellent. It is that they want a different look, a different personality." People are critical of the music they hear. They have personal likes and dislikes. Expect to hear plenty of negative comments along with the compliments. You cannot let rejection stop you if you truly want to make music for a living.

LEARNING & INNOVATION SKILLS

Technology is changing the way music is written. Composers no longer need to scribble down notes on paper. Today's composers can use software that records and writes down the music as it is played. For full orchestra pieces, the software keeps track of each instrument's part. Work that used to take months is now done quickly on a computer.

Even beginning musicians can write songs using software with prerecorded rhythms and melodies for different instruments. They can mix and match the pieces in endless combinations to create new music.

Software allows musicians to make high quality recordings of their music at home.

You have to sell your skills constantly. Permanent jobs are very rare. "You always need to be looking for the next gig, finding new ways to sell your talent, and practicing," says Tasha George-Hinnant. She suggests not being picky about the jobs you take. Beethoven may be your favorite, but playing sing-along tunes at the local senior center can put groceries on the table. You may not want to play in a church, but church work might allow you the freedom to look for other jobs.

Musicians sometimes play for small groups or even for people who just happen to walk by.

There were more than 186,000 professional musicians in the United States in 2008. The number is expected to grow about 8 percent by 2018. The U.S. Bureau of Labor Statistics expects most of these new jobs to come from churches. The Internet will also give musicians new opportunities to sell their music and show off their talents. But even with the Internet, there won't be enough jobs to go around. There will be more jobs for those who play instruments than for singers. This is also true today.

If you truly want to be a professional musician, here are some tips for finding work. Be prepared to move to a large city. Cities have more competition, but they also have more jobs available. Arrange to teach private lessons. You can advertise in the local music store. Play in churches, senior citizen homes, or high school assemblies. The pay for each performance will not be great. But the money will add up if you work a lot of jobs. Local ad agencies may need musicians to write and perform jingles. Event planners might hire musicians for trade shows or parties.

Keep track of how you spend your time as you pursue jobs. Time management and determination are just as important as talent. Be aggressive about jobs. Hunt down every opportunity. Create your own jobs. Talent does not guarantee success. Many talented people do not succeed in music. But good business practices and good music may add up to a great career.

Taylor Swift performs in a London concert.

SOME FAMOUS MUSICIANS

Louis Armstrong (1901–1971) was one of the most influential jazz artists of all time. He was born in New Orleans, Louisiana, and learned to play the cornet as a teenager. By the time he was 25, he had switched to trumpet. Later, he also became known as a singer.

Ludwig van Beethoven (1770–1827) is thought by many to be the greatest composer in the history of classical music. He was born in Germany and started playing and composing music as a child.

Michael Jackson (1958–2009) was a pop star by the time he was 12 years old. He began his career as the lead singer of the Jackson 5. He went on to become the most successful musician in the world, with solo albums such as *Off the Wall* and *Thriller*.

Beyoncé Knowles (1981–) first made it big as the lead singer of the R&B group Destiny's Child. She left the group and released her first solo album in 2003. It became a huge hit. Each one of her albums has sold millions of copies. In 2010, she won a record six Grammy awards for her album *I Am . . . Sasha Fierce* and its hit song "Single Ladies (Put a Ring on It)."

Taylor Swift (1989–) is one of today's most successful pop singers. She learned to play guitar when she was 12 years old and soon began writing songs. She released her first album when she was just 16. In 2010, she became the youngest artist ever to win the Grammy Award for Album of the Year.

Hank Williams (1923–1953) was the first country musician to become widely popular. He started playing guitar when he was 8 years old and made his first radio appearance when he was 13. He was known for his unique voice and emotional lyrics. More than 30 of his songs were top-10 hits.

GLOSSARY

audition (aw-DIH-shuhn) a performance that a musician gives in the hopes of winning a job

Broadway (BRAWD-way) a street in New York City that is the center of a world-famous theater district

composer (kuhm-POH-zur) person who writes music

conductor (kuhn-DUHK-tur) person who plans a performance and leads a band or orchestra

gigs (GIGZ) performing jobs

grant (GRANT) money given by a government or organization to fund new art projects

performance (pur-FOR-muhnss) a musical event

rehearsal (ri-HUR-suhl) a practice session that occurs before a performance

scales (SKAYLZ) series of notes within a range of music that sound good together

unions (YOON-yuhnz) organizations of employees that bargain with employers for benefits and pay requirements

FOR MORE INFORMATION

BOOKS

Ardley, Neil. *A Young Person's Guide to Music.* New York: DK Publishing, 2005.

Ball, Heather. *Magnificent Women in Music*. Toronto, Ontario: Second Story Press, 2006.

Nathan, Amy. *The Young Musician's Survival Guide: Tips from Teens and Pros.* New York: Oxford University Press, 2008.

Rauf, Don, and Monique Vescia. *Pop Musician.* New York: Ferguson, 2008.

WEB SITES

Dallas Symphony Orchestra—DSO Kids
www.dsokids.com/
Play games and learn more about music and musicians.

Library of Congress Performing Arts Encyclopedia
www.loc.gov/performingarts/index.html
Learn about many different kinds of music and the musicians who created it.

National Museum of American History—Music in the Museum
americanhistory.si.edu/collections/music.cfm
Read about the history of music and musical instruments in America.

INDEX

ABOUT THE AUTHOR

Barbara Somervill writes books about science, careers, and people. She loves listening to music but admits that she cannot play an instrument or sing a note. As a young woman, she worked backstage for a theater company and loved working on the musicals. "Working with talented musicians taught me how much work is involved in putting a show together," she says. "When the conductor raises his baton and the orchestra plays the overture, there is a hum of excitement in the air. There's nothing quite like it."